W9-CQZ-304

Staying Safe at School

School is meant to be a safe environment in which you can learn from your teachers and fellow students.

Staying Safe at School

Donna Chaiet

THE ROSEN PUBLISHING GROUP, INC.

NEW YORK

The author makes no representations or warranties, actual or im-
plied, as to the effectiveness or appropriateness of verbal or physical
techniques because it is impossible to predict the variables in any
given situation. The use of physical force in self-defense is a response
option only when your life is in imminent danger and risk of physical
injury is present. The laws regarding use of physical force in self-
defense vary from locality to locality, state to state, and country to
country, and the techniques described in this book may not conform
to your locality's legal standard. In order to best learn and understand the techniques described in this book, "hands on" training and
practice are necessary.

Published in 1995 by The Rosen Publishing Group, Inc.
29 East 21st Street, New York, NY 10010

First Edition

Manufactured in the United States of America.

Library of Congress Cataloging-in-Publication Data
Chaiet, Donna.
  Staying safe at school / Donna Chaiet.
    p. cm. — (The get prepared library of violence prevention
  for young women)
    Includes bibliographical references and index.
    Summary: Uses real-life examples to illustrate how to handle
  unwanted touching, verbal abuse, physical violence, and other
  potentially dangerous situations at school.
    ISBN 0-8239-1864-5
    1. Young women—Crimes against—Prevention—Juvenile
  literature.   2. Violent crimes—Prevention—Juvenile literature.
  3. School violence—Prevention—Juvenile literature.   4. Sexual
  harassment in education—Juvenile literature.   [1. Teenage girls—
  Crimes against.   2. Crime prevention.   3. Self-defense.
  4. Safety.]   I. Title.   II. Series: Chaiet, Donna.   Get prepared
  library of violence prevention for young women.
  HV6250.4.W65C523   1995
  613.6′0835′2—dc20   95-8493
                                                                   CIP
                                                                    AC

Contents

Introduction

There are many myths about personal safety and self-defense. Most of these myths come from the media: both entertainment (television and movies) and the reporting of violence on news shows and in newspapers. In a typical fictional scenario, the female character is alone and near a dark alley or in an underground parking lot. A large man leaps out at her. She either (1) cowers in fear and is victimized or (2) tries to run away but trips and is victimized. Real life is very different.

✓ Violations occur in many different forms, from people speaking to us in

Unwanted touching is just one type of violation.

inappropriate ways, to people touching our bodies without our permission,
to outright physical attacks or assaults.
✓ Violations occur in familiar settings.
✓ Violations occur with people we know.
✓ Violations can happen to anyone.
✓ Violations can often be avoided,
  deescalated, or dealt with once they
  begin.

In addition, younger women are fre-
quently targeted for sexual assault. A 1992   **7**

study, *Rape in America—A Report to the Nation*, conducted by the National Victim Center and the Crime Victims Research and Treatment Center, found that 29 percent of all rapes occurred when the victim was less than 11 years old, and another 32 percent occurred between the ages of 11 and 17. Moreover, numerous magazines and newspapers have featured stories on the increasing problem of teens, guns, and school violence. A recent New York *Newsday* cover story on school violence reported that 82 handguns, 43 air guns, 676 knives, and 558 box cutters and other dangerous instruments were confiscated in New York City schools during the first six months of the 1993–94 school year.

Even though teen violence is prevalent, personal safety is accessible to all. Everyone can learn to be their own first line of personal safety. Learning personal safety is learning to become more self-reliant in an increasingly violent culture.◆

When you were a child, your parents tried to keep you safe by teaching you strict rules about dealing with people. Now that you are older, the rules are less clear.

chapter 1

Basic Safety Rules

Some of you may have been exposed to safety programs when you were children. During those programs you were taught very firm rules, such as:

- ✓ Don't talk to strangers.
- ✓ Don't take anything from a stranger.
- ✓ Don't go anywhere with a stranger.

When you were a child, these rules probably served you well.

As you get older, creating a list of safety rules becomes more challenging. Clearly, there is no magic list of rules that will grant you perfect safety. However, there are

Certain settings, such as a relatively empty playing field, allow you to be more vulnerable than others.

some guidelines that can enhance your ability to stay safe. What is important to understand about the rules listed below is the underlying safety concept. The list is not intended to be complete; adapt it to your neighborhood and supplement your own safety code.

✓ **Be Aware.**

Pay attention to your environment. Try at all costs to avoid dangerous situations that make you more vulnerable to attack. For example, being in a setting where you are isolated or you cannot see **11** around you makes you an easier target for assault. In a school setting, bathrooms and locker rooms may have limited visibility from certain spots. A deserted hallway after school or an empty field or track area are other examples. Avoid such situations whenever possible. If you must be isolated, let someone know where you are going and when you expect to return. Increase your level of alertness and make continuous sweeps around your field of vision. If you see someone approaching or feel that something is not quite right, leave the area immediately and go to a more public or populated area.

✓ **Walk with Confidence.**

Your carriage can make you look like an easier target for a crime. The body language that is associated with being selected for crime is looking tired, lost, disoriented or inattentive. Body language that reflects this mood is looking down (tired) or looking up as if to read street signs (lost or disoriented). Avoid this behavior by walking with your head up and shoulders back. Walk with purpose and direction.

Traveling to and from school—whether across the street or across
the state—involves safety risks.

✓ **Know your boundaries.**

Boundaries refer to the physical space that surrounds you. The farther you are physically from a potentially dangerous situation, the more time you have to react and the more choices you have about how you react. Be particularly aware if someone is getting too close to you, is following you, or won't leave you alone. In a school setting this might mean avoiding or staying far away from groups of students who follow you, people who verbally harass you by making fun of you or taunting you, or someone who constantly stares at you. It might also mean keeping your physical distance from a person who constantly tries to touch or hug you.

✓ **Enforce your boundaries.**

Criminals are looking for easy marks, people who will not put up any resistance. Behavior that marks you as an easy target is overniceness in a situation that does not call for niceness. Criminals often "test" potential victims to gauge how they will react to an intrusion into their boundaries.

For example, a criminal might sit down

beside you while you are waiting for the school bus and ask you personal questions. If you answer, you are behaving in a way that indicates cooperation and an easy target. Many of you might talk to such a person because you don't want to hurt his feelings or because you believe that you have to be nice to everyone. Giving information about yourself during this "testing" process marks you as compliant. You can enforce your boundaries by getting up and leaving or telling the person to leave you alone. Enforcing your boundaries by creating physical distance or verbally communicating that you want the person to stop sends a message to the criminal that you will not be an easy target.

✓ **Avoid drugs and alcohol.**

Using drugs or alcohol may increase the likelihood that you will be targeted for assault. Drugs and alcohol limit your ability to make decisions and also make you physically less capable. What might seem like an unwise choice when you are sober seems okay when you are high. Accepting a ride home with someone who has been drink-

Drugs and alcohol cloud your judgment and dull your senses.

ing or with someone you do not know are further examples of behavior that might put you in danger. It is also more dangerous to be with people who are under the influence of both drugs and alcohol. People who use drugs (particularly crack cocaine) and alcohol are likely to be violent. Their inhibitions are lowered, and their decision-making capacity is greatly limited.

✓ **Dress with an eye toward your personal safety.**

A growing area of concern is attacks based on clothing. Every neighborhood is different, and fashion changes very quickly.

A good rule of thumb is to avoid clothing, either by color or fashion, that might be gang-associated or encourage violence. Many schools have dress codes in attempts to decrease the violence based on dress styles. You may feel that this limits your ability to express yourself (and it may!), but it also may mean the difference between being a victim or not.

✓ **Stay calm if a weapon is involved.**

If you are threatened with a weapon, you are in a dangerous situation. Movies and television tend to "clean up" the damage that a gun or knife does to the human body. The actual results are devastating. Breathe deeply and exhale. Move slowly and deliberately and speak in a level tone of voice. Negotiate by offering property, if you have it. No property is worth risking your life for. Convince the person that the weapon is not needed to complete the crime.

If you live in a neighborhood marked by persistent violence and you hear gunfire, drop to the ground immediately. Try to get to cover or concealment if at all possible.◆

chapter 2

The School Setting

*a*s a student, you face a challenging environment from a safety perspective because you deal with so many different people in any given day. On the way to school you may interact with a bus driver, people on the street, your friends, teachers, school nurses, and doctors. Some of these people you may know very well; some of them may be mere acquaintances; and some of them may be total strangers.

Also, you have different relationships with each of these people. For example, you and your friends are peers, but you and your teachers are in a superior/subordinate

School presents a particular challenge to safety because you come into contact with so many different people.

relationship. You have an ongoing relationship with a coach or teacher, but you interact only occasionally with a doctor or nurse.

How does this all relate to your safety? Most assaults occur with people we know. It is important to consider what kind of relationship you have with the assailant, as well as the type of violation that is occurring. The way you handle a situation with someone with whom you interact once a year might be different than in a situation with someone with whom you have an ongoing relationship.

The type of relationship you have with people affects how you react if they violate your boundaries.

It is also important to understand how being female in a school setting can affect your safety. American culture tends to socialize females in a way that hampers their ability to take care of themselves. For example, girls are told that speaking loudly, saying what they want, and not cooperating are unfeminine behaviors. But people with these "unfeminine" qualities are less likely to be selected for violence. And people who respond to an assault by being loud and assertive are the most likely to stop a dangerous situation once it begins. New data re-

Many teenaged girls have low self-esteem. They may believe that it
is acceptable for someone to put them down.

ported in the *American Journal of Public Health* (November 1993) found that forceful verbal resistance (screaming or yelling) helped avoid rape.

Similarly, girls are taught that being physically active and playing sports are unladylike. Sometimes girls are told that they are ugly, stupid, fat, thin; even when no one says these things, some girls believe them anyway. If you have low self-esteem, it may lead you to believe that it is okay for people to put you down. But if you grow used to being put down, you may fail to recognize it as a signal of a potentially more dangerous situation.

Peer pressure also forces teens into conforming behavior. Being able to take care of yourself means identifying what is okay for you, even if it is different from the group's decision. Being able to realize your individual needs and express them at the risk of looking stupid is a challenge. If you can face this challenge, however, you can improve your ability to stay safe.◆

chapter 3

Dealing with Unwanted Touching

Aneesa

Aneesa trained on the cross-country team with Coach Bob at Cook County High School. Aneesa was new to Cook County. Her parents had just broken up. Her father drank, and Aneesa often heard loud arguments. Never knowing what to do during these incidents, she retreated into saying nothing. As a result, Aneesa was shy, introverted, and had trouble expressing herself.

Everyone spoke highly of Coach Bob. Aneesa thought Bob was a little weird but wasn't sure why. When she mentioned this to an older teammate, she was told that she

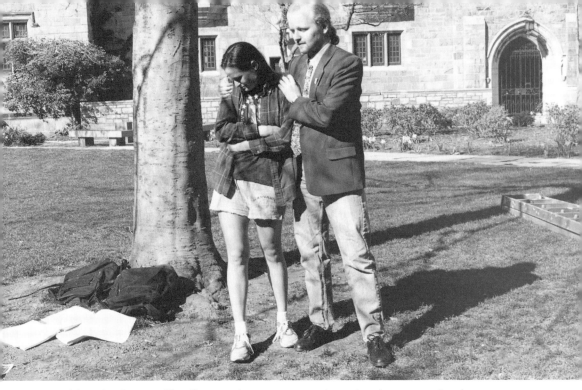

Your instincts will tell you when someone is acting inappropriately toward you.

was too young to appreciate how great Bob was.

Aneesa saw Coach Bob at practice every day, and they met periodically to go over her times and training schedule. Bob always gave her a big hug and sometimes squeezed her buttocks. He did this with all the girls, and no one seemed to mind. In fact, they adored Bob.

Aneesa had a bad day one Friday. She was scheduled to meet with Bob that afternoon and didn't feel like one of his smothering hugs. When she got to his office, she

put her hand out in front of her and said,

"I'm sick. Don't hug me today." Bob looked hurt and disappointed. He said, "A hug a day keeps people healthy." Before she could put her hand back up, Bob gave her a very tight hug. It definitely did not brighten her day.

Aneesa began avoiding Bob as much as possible. She started resenting him but hid her feelings. Sometimes her avoidance tactics worked, and sometimes they didn't. Bob's behavior didn't change no matter how much physical distance she put between them. She liked training, and the more she trained with Bob the more she realized that he was a talented coach and could help her a lot. Aneesa decided she had no choice but to tolerate his behavior. After her first season on the track team, she barely noticed it.

Do you think Coach Bob's behavior was a violation?

Have you ever been touched in ways that made you uncomfortable?

People who are in a position of authority may feel that they have the right to treat you in an intimate, demeaning, or violent way. Often, their behavior is cloaked in very small violations that seem to be okay but then progress into something else. These people coerce you into engaging in behavior that you normally would not do, but do for the sake of the relationship. These people are abusing their power.

Most sexual violence is committed by people we know. *Rape in America—A Report to the Nation* found that 75 percent of the time the victim knew her attacker.

Any unwanted touching of our bodies is wrong. We have the right to prevent, and we can prevent, unwanted touching, even by people we know. If we can learn the basic skills of safety in nonlife-threatening situations and we can learn to tune in to our instincts and intuition, we will also be prepared to deal with someone who is a stranger and means to hurt, rape, or kill us.

One of the foundations of personal safety is a concept called "boundaries." The concept of boundaries can be described in both physical and emotional terms. If you know your boundaries, you are paying attention to your surroundings and, even

Sometimes people violate our boundaries.

more important, to your feelings and emotions.

Your physical boundaries can be described as your comfort zone. Most of you can relate to having a certain space bubble that marks a comfortable and appropriate distance for talking with friends, for example. Generally North American culture dictates a one- to two-foot distance—close enough so that you could extend your arm and touch the other person, but not so close that you could kiss without having to lean in.

We learn our comfort zone from our culture. We also learn about boundaries from our family. Some families are physically affectionate and members touch each other all the time. Other family members rarely touch one another.

Note that there is nothing intrinsically good or bad about any one boundary system. It is what it is. Most of the time what we have learned suits us fine in our daily experiences. Sometimes, however, our boundaries are violated, and we are not sure if that is okay or not. An example of boundary violation are Coach Bob's hugs.

What could Aneesa do in this situation? Does she have to tolerate the coach's behavior? Every person is different and every situation is different. However, there is a simple process that can be applied when you are being touched without permission.

Step One: Pay attention to what is happening and identify the problem.

✓ Almost from the beginning of her relationship with Coach Bob, Aneesa thought he was weird. She felt uncomfortable. Some people may think that Aneesa was jumping to conclusions or not giving Bob a chance. In fact, she had very good instincts and should have listened to them.

✓ The first thing for Aneesa to do around people who make her uncomfortable is to increase her alertness when they are nearby. That doesn't mean that she has to act paranoid; we all know how to look and act alert without being paranoid. For example, when you ride your bicycle in a city or densely populated area, you stay very aware of the traffic. That isn't being paranoid; it is being alert.

✓ The second thing Aneesa should do is identify what exactly Coach Bob does that makes her uncomfortable. We can't make people change their personalities, but we can ask them to change behavior. Clearly it is Bob's touching that makes Aneesa uncomfortable. It doesn't matter that he does the same thing to all the other girls and it is okay with them. If the behavior is not okay with Aneesa, that is all that matters.

Step Two: Address the problem.

✓ Problems do not go away on their own; the sooner we address them, the better. It will be a challenge speaking to Coach Bob because Aneesa needs a relationship with him if she wants to be on the cross-country team.

Coach Bob has a position of power and can affect Aneesa's daily life.

✓ The best way to address the situation is to plan for it. Think of it in the same terms as preparing for a test or for a tryout for a school team or play. The better prepared you are, the better your chances of success.

✓ Visualize what the encounter might look like—at his office, on the track, before or after practice? Prepare what you will say and how you will say it. Try to imagine what he might answer and how you could best respond.

✓ Choose a setting that maximizes your outcome. If Aneesa knows that after practice Coach Bob is a little hurried to get home, that would not be the best time to address him. Perhaps a better time would be before a practice or during a lunch period.

✓ Get the person's undivided attention. The goal is to have him realize that you need to discuss something important. For example, Aneesa might say, "Coach Bob, I need to talk to you

Body language is an important part of how we communicate. Use
yours to enhance your safety.

about something very important. Is this a good time?"

✓ State what is happening. Aneesa could then use a formula for easier communication. This formula can be used in many situations and works well. She could say, "Coach Bob, I feel very uncomfortable when you hug me and squeeze my buttocks. Please stop."

The most important elements of this sentence are that Aneesa tells Bob that she is uncomfortable and owns her own feelings. She didn't say, "Bob, you make me uncomfortable." Putting the emphasis on how *you* feel helps take people off the defensive because you are not attacking them. Next, she identifies what exactly bothers her. It is important that Aneesa stick to describing behavior rather than naming a personality defect. Telling Bob that his lecherous ways are disgusting would not work very well. The last thing she does is tell him in clear language what she wants. Using words like "please" and "thank you" are appropriate with people you know and like. Being respectful (if you can) makes people less defensive. Aneesa also makes sure to use directive language. "Stop" and "Don't touch me anymore" are examples of directive language.

Bob may have a number of reactions to Aneesa's statement. He could acknowledge her feelings and say that he will stop his behavior. People who are sensitive and listen to what we are asking for often respect our request. However, sometimes people don't listen, and if they don't "hear" what we say, obviously they can't respect it. Bob might say something like, "What is your problem? All the other girls love the affection and attention." Aneesa could answer by repeating her request. This is not a debate over other people's boundaries; it is a discussion of Aneesa's boundaries and what she wants. Therefore, Aneesa should simply repeat herself: "I am uncomfortable when you touch my buttocks. Please stop." Repetition often works. Some people need to hear a message more than once for it to sink in or for them to realize that you mean what you say.

It can be useful to write down a description of any abusive behavior, sexual or otherwise.

Coach Bob seems like the kind of coach who wants his athletes to be happy and to perform well. Directive, clear, and non-threatening language should get the result that Aneesa wants. However, what if Coach Bob escalates the situation? He might do this by raising his voice and getting angry, or he might do it more subtly by making Aneesa feel guilty about her request. Aneesa is not responsible for Coach Bob's feelings. If he gets angry or feels hurt, that is his problem; as an adult he should be able to deal with those emotions without compromising Aneesa's.

If Coach Bob threatens to kick her off the team, Aneesa obviously has a different and even more challenging situation on her hands. A lot of teens (and women) are reluctant to address people like Coach Bob for fear of negative consequences, like not starting on the team or losing a job or getting a bad grade. Making choices about what is important to you is very difficult. Some of you may think that Coach Bob's behavior was not that bad and didn't need to be addressed. Even Aneesa got used to it after the first season. However, Coach Bob's behavior *is* inappropriate. Such behavior in the workplace is legally defined as sexual harassment. It is not acceptable in the workplace, and it is not acceptable in a school. If you are being touched by a teacher or school administrator, let another teacher or your guidance counselor know about it. It is very possible that your school has a reporting system for this kind of behavior. It is a good idea to keep a diary of all of the times you have been touched without explicit permission. Handwritten notes that were made the day of the event can be very persuasive, particularly if other people knew of or saw the touchings.

Clearly the decision about reporting this kind of behavior has to be made by the person being touched. If Aneesa's perform-ance on the track team suffered because she was unable to concentrate, or she had to avoid practices because Coach Bob's behavior made her so uncomfortable, she might have had no choice but to discuss his behavior.

Aneesa also has to decide if the potential consequences of confronting Coach Bob are worth the risk. Are there other teams she could train with and still get the same exposure to college recruiters? Are there other opportunities to get noticed, such as participating in summer sports programs? Could she train without Coach Bob and still compete in local events? How important is running cross country?

Aneesa might also talk to her mother or father. Parents and other trusted adults can help you. She could use a variation on the formula for easier communication and let her mother or father know that there is something important she needs to discuss with them. Aneesa can even preset a boundary and tell them what she needs in advance. For example, "I have something important to discuss. It is very important to me that you let me speak without interrupting and that you don't overreact to what I am saying." Many parents, told that a teacher or coach was touching a daughter's body, would have hit the ceiling and gone down to the school in about two seconds. That probably isn't the best way to handle it, although it might feel really great. If you can enlist the support of one or both of your parents, perhaps they could join you during the discussion with Coach Bob. (It is possible that a parent could take care of the entire situation. This book assumes that there will be times when your parents, peers, siblings, police, or security guards are not available. However, getting people to help us during difficult situations is a good form of personal safety.)◆

chapter 4

Coping with Verbal Abuse

Sometimes a person in authority does not touch you in a way that makes you uncomfortable, but talks to you in a demeaning manner. Words can cross boundaries as easily as physical touching. Boundary violations can also occur on an emotional level.

Susan

Susan is a 13-year-old entering middle school. An exam is required with Dr. Johns, the school physician. Susan was scheduled to see Dr. Johns after gym class. Because the girls' showers were out of order, she toweled off, got dressed, and ran off to her appointment.

Susan arrived at Dr. Johns' office late and apologized. Dr. Johns angrily told her to step into his office and take off her shirt. She waited for him to leave while she undressed. Her regular doctor always did, but Dr. Johns stayed. Susan was a little self-conscious and didn't like the way he stared at her, but she wanted to get the exam over with. She quickly undid her blouse. Dr. Johns checked her throat, her nose, and her ears. He then put on his stethoscope and touched her breast to put the instrument underneath. Susan immediately froze. She couldn't believe he had touched her body without any warning. He then told her she had horrible body odor. Susan was very embarrassed. She did not know what to do or say. When the exam was finished, she put her shirt back on and quickly left the office.

Do you think that Dr. Johns violated Susan's boundaries? What could Susan have done?

Let's look at some of her options. First, if Susan does not like seeing a doctor other

Hurtful words can violate boundaries as easily as physical acts.

than her family doctor, she could ask whether a note from him would suffice. She might also have asked some older students how they liked Dr. Johns. If he had a reputation as being mean or gruff, she might want to avoid seeing him if she could. If Susan had to see the school doctor, she could have asked if a nurse could be present during the exam. This kind of behavior usually does not occur with a witness.

What were some of her options once the exam began? Susan's first tip-off that things might not go well occurred when Dr. Johns **41** was angry with her for being late. If she felt that his anger was going to interfere with his professional conduct, she could set a boundary. She could say, "You appear angry. I'm sorry I was late. Do you want me to reschedule the appointment?" Obviously, it is okay for Dr. Johns to be angry. No one likes to be kept waiting. However, he should be able to examine Susan without demeaning her.

The next thing that happened was that Dr. Johns asked her to undress in front of him. Susan knows that is not what doctors do. They always leave or put up a screen for privacy. Susan can set another boundary by telling Dr. Johns what she wants. "I will not undress until you leave" or "Please send in a nurse" or "I know that I should have privacy when I undress; if you do not leave I will let the school principal know what you are doing."

In addition to touching Susan in a sudden manner, he also spoke disrespectfully. This kind of language is a violation; no one has the right to talk to you in a demeaning way. If the doctor felt that Susan's hygiene was truly poor, he could have talked to her professionally and respectfully after the exam. Susan then could have explained that the showers were broken and she was unable to bathe. (That is also setting a good boundary.)

The last option (which Susan could have exercised at any point during the examination) was to get up and leave. Leaving would be setting the ultimate boundary. Susan does not have to stay in an exam with a physician who is making her feel uncomfortable.

Finally, Susan had a choice at the end of the examination. She could have told the doctor that it is inappropriate for him to speak to her in that tone of voice. If he has something to say, he can say it in a respectful and professional way. Susan also has choices about reporting Dr. Johns' conduct to the school or his licensing agency. His behavior was totally unprofessional and needed to be addressed in a formal way.◆

Bathrooms and locker rooms may be isolated areas after school or during classes. It is good to practice your safety precautions when entering any potentially deserted or isolated area.

chapter 5

Dealing with
School Violence

*R*ebecca, an 11th-grader, founded a
student group called the "Women's
Room," dedicated to promoting women's
rights. Rebecca often stays late after
classes to organize events for her club. One
day after school Rebecca went into the
bathroom. She did not like using the school
bathrooms because girls sometimes hung
out there and smoked cigarettes and drank
alcohol. However, she knew she was going
to be staying late and couldn't wait until
she got home.

As Rebecca entered the L-shaped bathroom, she went to the back where the
sinks were to see if anyone was there. **45**

Looking around the corner, she saw two girls and two boys drinking. Rebecca momentarily froze in her steps. She could not believe that there were boys in the bathroom.

One of the girls addressed her first, "Hey, 'Becca. How about a smoke?" Rebecca did not drink or smoke and politely declined. The other girl continued, "Looking good . . . great boots . . ." and they all cracked up laughing. Rebecca decided to abandon the idea of using the bathroom, but as she turned to leave one of the boys blocked her exit. Now she was really scared. She stopped breathing and felt her knees get weak. She knew she was cornered and that no one would hear her screaming from the bathroom.

The boy who had blocked her path told her that she looked really great, although her short hair made her look a little boyish. He asked her if she was a lesbian and if she had ever had sex with a guy. Rebecca intuitively knew that answering was not likely to help her and that he was trying to intimidate and shock her. Whatever was the case, his language was paralyzing her with fear. She couldn't say a word. He then went to unzip his fly and told her he was going to force her to have oral sex with him.

Rebecca decided that there was no way she was going to be sexually assaulted by this jerk. She walked over to him slowly as if she were going to cooperate. She backed him up into a stall and pretended that she was going to touch him. Instead she quickly kicked him in the shin and pushed him into the toilet. She then ran out of the bathroom toward the janitor's office as fast as she could.

Rebecca's confrontation with sexual violence is shocking. It is shocking to think that a place that is supposed to be private and safe, like a bathroom, could in fact be a place where you can be attacked. It is also shocking that people Rebecca knew as acquaintances would try to hurt her. It is important to realize that familiar people can also assault you.

Just because Rebecca went into a bathroom where she knew girls smoked cigarettes did not mean that she wanted to be victimized. She was doing nothing more than trying to use the bathroom. Rebecca might have tried ways to make a potentially dangerous situation safer. For example, she might have asked a friend or teacher to go with her. But Rebecca did nothing wrong, and it would be unfair to blame her for the actions of drunken teenagers who meant her harm.

Rebecca's inability to move or speak is a common reaction to fear and danger. Called the freeze response, it is a natural biological reaction to fear and danger. Our bodies respond in predictable ways. Often there is a sharp intake of breath and a corresponding inability to move or react. One of the best ways to break through this freeze is to exhale and breathe as deeply as possible. We want to avoid staying frozen and we want to move into another natural response called the fight/flight response. This occurs when adrenaline and other hormones are released into the bloodstream and create a biological phenomenon that makes us stronger and faster.

Rebecca could have broken the freeze

response in another way, by yelling very loudly. Whenever we exhale, we are forced to inhale, and yelling is a very dramatic way to exhale. Even though Rebecca knew that yelling wouldn't bring help, it is a response that also works to show fighting spirit and prepare you to do whatever you need to do. She did not need to shriek or beg, but she should set a very clear and loud boundary: "Leave me alone. I don't want any trouble. Back off!" She also could have very quickly exited the bathroom the instant she saw she wasn't alone.

Rebecca might also have tried another verbal self-defense strategy, such as lying. For example, "Hey, I don't want any problems. I know that Mrs. Smith is on her way in here." Letting people know that you are aware and responding to the situation, not panicking or begging, sets you up as a nonvictim. Another strategy is to ask questions, such as, "I know you. Your name is Rick. Right? Doesn't my brother hang out with your brother?" Questions are a really good way to defuse a situation. They make you look aware and alert and tend to interrupt the flow of the assault. This forces the assailant to create a new plan.

Rebecca did a lot of things well, and it is not our place to second-guess her judgment. Even though Rebecca was freezing up and was really scared, she managed to keep her wits about her and assess what was going on. She was able to identify that the teens were bullying her and was able to trick the attacker into believing she was cooperating. Cooperation was exactly what he expected. That was how she could get him into a stall and not alert him that she was going to make a move.

Using physical self-defense techniques is always the last resort. The first goal is to avoid the danger; the second goal is to try to talk your way out of the problem. If those two strategies fail and you are being confronted with a life/death situation or rape, physical self-defense is an option. My self-defense class, Prepare Self-Defense, trains young women in simple and easy-to-use techniques. The philosophy of the program is based on four important points:

Prepare Self-Defense teaches young women to use their voices,
their wits, and their physical strength to deflect or defeat attackers.

✓ **Men and women are attacked differently.** Men are attacked in face-to-face
confrontations often referred to as ter-
ritorial fights. Women are confronted
with overwhelming attacks, either verbal or physical, and they are confronted by predatory attacks. These
are more sneaky, surprise attacks,
usually from behind. In the case of
sexual assault and rapes, it may involve the victim's being thrown to the
ground.   *51*

✓ **Men and women are physically different.** Men have more upper body strength, and women have most of their body strength in their lower bodies.

✓ **Men and women are socially conditioned differently.** Women are brought up to be passive, compliant, and quiet; boys are encouraged to be loud, physical, and aggressive.

✓ **You will respond as you are trained to respond.** The only way to learn physical skills is to do them. Training in realistic scenarios is the best way to ensure that your body will remember these techniques beyond what you can memorize.

What all this means is that it is possible to learn physical techniques in short-term training. You do not have to train for years in order to be able to take care of yourself if your life is in danger.

Training in martial arts is wonderful, teaches discipline, and is great physical conditioning. If you are going to train in a martial art to develop practical self-defense knowledge, do some research and speak to students who train there. Make sure it is female-friendly—that the instructors recognize that techniques that work for men may not work as well for women, who are typically smaller and have less upper body strength. Visit a few schools and watch classes. Among disadvantages to training in martial arts are the facts that it takes many years to become competent and that verbal self-defense skills are typically not taught.

Prepare Self-Defense trains students by allowing them to learn and practice how they would respond verbally (using your voice) and physically (using your body) to an actual attack in role-playing scenarios with padded mock assailants. The more training you have, the more likely you are to succeed if you choose to resist, to fight back. If you do choose to fight back, however, you must do so with a 100 percent commitment. Fighting back is an option. There is no one right choice in an attack situation. Only you know what is the right choice, to fight or not, in a given situation.

If you do choose to fight back, be committed to the fight. This is called fighting spirit. If you have it, you are more likely to succeed. Respond quickly and decisively. Be unpredictable and ruthless. Make sure to target the most vulnerable parts of the attacker's body: eyes, throat, temple, nose, and chin on the upper body and the groin, knees, shins, and insteps on his lower body. Use environmental weapons such as pens, lamps, garbage can lids, dirt, sand, etc.; striking with or throwing these objects into the target areas is very effective.

If you end up on the ground, using your legs to kick is also very effective. Make sure that you stay on your side (not on your back) and keep your legs between you and the attacker. This ensures that your head is as far away as possible from his arms and legs. Target his groin or knee if possible. If he grabs one leg, try to kick his groin or knee with the other leg.

If you are confronted with a weapon and the attacker wants property, the best way to stay safe is to give over your property. However, if the attacker wants to abduct you or

If you decide to fight an attacker, you must fight with 100 percent of your strength and concentration. Self-defense classes can help prepare you for a physical assault.

kill you, choosing to fight immediately, before you are taken to a more isolated place, makes sense in a lot of situations. Yell loudly, bite his arm, grab his testicles, or kick his shins. Target his vulnerable areas. Be ruthless, and don't worry about hurting your attacker. If you are confronted with a group or gang, try to negotiate with the gang leader, or run away. The leader is the one who is doing all the talking. If you feel your life is in immediate danger and you choose a physical response, he is the person to deal with first. Very often, if the leader is confronted, the gang disperses.

It is important to note that there are no guarantees in using physical responses to violence and that using a physical response is most appropriate in life/death situations. The overwhelming majority of incidents that you will deal with in your life will not involve a weapon or a gang. Learning how to deal with these situations is certainly possible, and with a little practice you can learn to how stay safe.◆

Conclusion

Learning how to stay reasonably safe in the school setting is possible for all of you. Even though your school is a familiar environment, it will still serve you well to be aware of what is happening around you. Avoid isolated areas and trust your instincts. If something feels wrong, something probably is. Pay attention to your options and choices. Assess what is happening and address it as soon as possible. Use verbal self-defense strategies, and try to negotiate or talk your way out of the problem. If your life is in immediate danger, you can choose to fight back. Act decisively, swiftly, and ruthlessly, and then get to safety as soon as possible.◆

Glossary

assailant Person who commits a crime.

boundary Physical distance or an emotional limit that surrounds a person.

coercion Force used to make a person do something he does not want to do.

comfort zone Your own personal physical boundary.

directive language Words that clearly state what you want: Stop, Go away, Leave me alone, Back off.

femininity Behavior or traits associated with being female.

fight/flight syndrome Biological response in which adrenaline and other hormones are released into the bloodstream, enabling the person to fight or run away.

freeze response   Natural biological response to fear or danger that can paralyze a person.

internal awareness   Knowledge of your own thoughts and feelings.

nonvictim attitude   Body language, facial expression, and verbal traits that make you look confident and assured.

physical assault   Crime in which the victim is touched, beaten, or hit.

testing process   One of the first steps that criminals use to evaluate a victim; sometimes referred to as the interview process.

rape crisis center   Organization based in the community or a hospital with trained staff to assist women and men who have been raped or sexually assaulted.

sexual harassment   Behavior that includes unwanted touching or verbal intimidation.

sexual violence   Criminal behavior including rape, sexual assault, or violence or threats of violence to force a sexual act.

unwanted touching   Behavior in which one party physically touches another without permission.

violation   Broadly defined, includes physical violence, sexual violence, property crime, sexual harassment, and unwanted touching.

Resource List

General Information

ACLU Women's Rights Project
American Civil Liberties Union
132 West 43rd Street
New York, NY 10036

National Organization for Women (NOW)
1000 16th Street NW
Washington, DC 20036
202-331-0066

Women Plan Toronto
736 Bathurst St.
Toronto, Ontario M5S 2R4
416-588-9751

Information on Crime and Victimization

Crime Victims Counseling
P.O. Box 023003
Brooklyn, NY 11202-0060
718-875-5862

National Organization for Victim Assistance
1757 Park Road NW
Washington, DC 20010
800-879-6682

In Canada, call 1-800-VICTIMS (1-800-842-8467)

Rape Crisis Centers (For a nationwide listing of rape
    crisis centers, call the Washington, DC, Rape
    Crisis Center Hotline, 202-333-7273, or check
    the phone book for local information)

Ottawa Sexual Assault Support Centre Hotline
613-234-2266

Toronto Rape Crisis Centre Hotline
416-597-8808

Information on Self-Defense Training

Impact Personal Safety
19310 Ventura Boulevard
Tarzana, California 91356
818-757-3963

Prepare Self-Defense
25 West 43rd Street
New York, NY 10036
800-442-7273

Woman's Way Self Defense
512 Silver Spring Avenue
Silver Spring, MD 20910

In Canada, call Impact Personal Safety at 818-757-3963 for references to Canadian self-defense programs

For Further Reading

Bravo, Ellen, and Cassedy, Ellen. *The 9 to 5 Guide to Combatting Sexual Harassment.* New York: John Wiley & Sons, 1992.

Brownmiller, Susan. *Against Our Will: Men, Women, and Rape,* rev. ed. New York: Bantam Books, 1988.

Caignon and Groves. *Her Wits About Her.* New York: Harper and Row, 1987.

Cooney, Judith. *Coping with Sexual Abuse,* rev. ed. New York: Rosen Publishing Group, 1991.

Cooper, Jeff. *Principles of Personal Safety.* Colorado: Paladin Press.

Gilligan, Carol. *In a Different Voice: Psychological Theory and Women's Development.* Cambridge: Harvard University Press, 1982.

Kahaner, Ellen. *Growing Up Female,* rev. ed. New York: Rosen Publishing Group, 1991.

Langelan, Martha. *Back Off! How to Confront and Stop Sexual Harassment and Harasser.* New York: Simon & Schuster, 1993.

Parrot, Andrea. *Coping with Date Rape and Acquaintance Rape,* rev. ed. New York: Rosen Publishing Group, 1995.

Index

Acknowledgments

This book is dedicated to Karen Chasen, Executive Director at Prepare Self-Defense. Without her constant support, editorial eye, and sense of humor none of these books would have been completed. Many other people have taught me about self-defense and personal safety. Listing them all would take many pages. However, my deepest thanks go to Lisa Gaeta, Director of Impact Personal Safety, Los Angeles. Lastly, I want to thank my parents, who have always taught me to "be aware."

About the Author

Donna Chaiet, a practicing attorney in New York City, is the founder and President of Prepare, Inc. Prepare conducts personal safety programs that teach teenagers the verbal and physical skills required to defend themselves by training them to fight against a padded mock assailant. Ms. Chaiet is a recognized speaker and conducts safety/communication seminars for schools, community organizations, and Fortune 500 companies throughout the United States. Her frequent television appearances include CBS, NBC, ABC, WOR, FOX, Lifetime, Fox Cable, and New York 1.

Photo Credits

Cover, pp. 19. 20, 21, 27, 41, 51, 55 by Michael Brandt; pp. 7, 35 by Yung-Hee Chia; pp. 9, 11, 13, 16, 24, 32 by Kim Sonsky; pp. 2, 44 by Katherine Hsu

Design

Kim Sonsky